I Loved Her

By Shezza Ansloos

Illustrated by Kimberly McKay-Fleming

Pemmican Publications gratefully acknowledges the assistance accorded to its publishing program
by the Manitoba Arts Council, the Province of Manitoba – Department of Culture, Heritage and
Tourism, Canada Council for the Arts and Canadian Heritage – Canada Book Fund.

Design and Layout by Relish Design Studio Ltd.
Printed and Bound in Canada.

First printing: 2010

Library and Archives Canada Cataloguing in Publication

Ansloos, Shezza

        I loved her / by Shezza Ansloos ; illustrations by

Kimberly McKay-Fleming.

ISBN 978-1-894717-59-5

        I. McKay-Fleming, Kimberly, 1968- II. Title.

PS8601.N55I3 2010   jC813'.6   C2010-905316-8

PEMMICAN
PUBLICATIONS
INC.

Committed to the promotion of Metis culture and heritage

150 Henry Ave., Winnipeg,
Manitoba, R3B 0J7, Canada

www.pemmican.mb.ca

To my Grandma Lavallee, and in loving memory of Florence Linda Thompson.

Sometimes when I am alone in my room I think about my grandmother. Her picture is on my dresser beside the bed. I keep it there so I will never forget what she looked like.

My dad said that my grandmother is not with us anymore. He told me she is in heaven now. When I look at her picture, I remember the things we used to do together.

4

I used to visit my grandmother on Saturdays. I would race to her front door and knock. I would yell, "Kokum! It's me!"

She would open the door and smile the biggest smile anybody could ever smile. She would hug me tightly and say, "I'm glad you're here, dear."

She smelled like roses.

I loved her.

I used to sit with my grandmother at the piano. She would play happy jigs and rollicking songs, her long fingers dancing over the keys, her nails making clicking sounds as she tapped out her tunes. We would sway and sing out loudly like we were the stars of the show.

I loved her.

8

I would eat breakfast at her kitchen table, with mounds of food before me – fried eggs and bacon, porridge with brown sugar and milk, buttery toast and orange juice. She smiled, sitting there in her yellow and blue apron as I ate.

"You'll grow good and strong," she said.

I loved her.

We liked taking walks together in the garden. Her white gardening shoes were stained green at the toes. I would put on my rubber boots and clomp along beside her. The lilies, daisies, ferns and hollyhocks fluttered and waved as we passed by. She would stop and introduce me to them all, like they were old friends.

I loved her.

Sometimes my family would take her for a drive on a Sunday afternoon. I would sit beside her in the back seat. I would hold her hand and touch the furrowed wrinkles that were there from years of hard work and sunshine.

She would wink and pass me a green peppermint like it was our little secret. I could hear her pleasant voice in my ear as she hummed and looked out the window.

I loved her.

I could hardly wait for a rainy day with my grandmother. We used to open the window just to hear the sound of the rain falling and smell the fresh scent of wet grass. We would drink hot chocolate and play Parcheesi, checkers, rummy or crazy eights all afternoon. She would never cheat. Her eyes would sparkle and laugh, and she never made you feel bad for winning or losing.

I loved her.

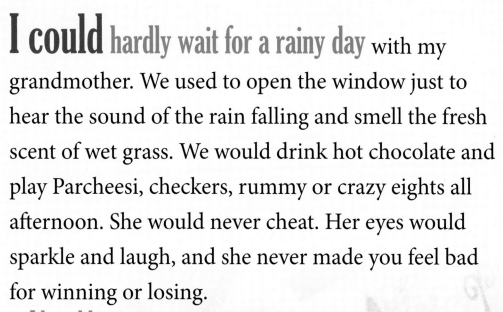

I used to help her make bread. She would move around the kitchen making it look so easy—just a little flour, eggs, salt, yeast, oil and water mixed together. The smell of fresh bread filled the house. We would eat it warm from the oven with butter and honey, our fingers dripping sweet goodness.

I loved her.

I used to sleep in her bed on nights when I was afraid of the dark. She would make room for me and my teddy bear, saying, "I'm glad you're here to keep me company. I can't sleep either."

She would tell me stories about when she was a little girl, like when she stood up to the older boys who pulled her braids. As I lay in her arms and listened, the shadows and noises of the house did not scare me anymore. Somehow I felt braver when I was with her.

I loved her.

20

I used to sit on her bed and watch her comb her hair and put on her makeup. All of her trinkets on the dressing table—lipstick, powder, perfume, rings and beads—shone like candy. She would powder my nose and dot my cheeks with blush, saying, "What a beautiful girl you are."

I loved her.

I used to watch her knit. Her fingers moved in mysterious twists and turns, the needles clicking and clacking, the bright-coloured yarn weaving its way into shapes I could recognize – slippers, mittens, toques and scarves. She could create love and warmth from bits of string.

I loved her.

We used to drink tea out of fancy cups, acting all prim and proper. The teacups were white with delicate lavender flowers, and they tinkled when you stirred the tea. I always put two sugar cubes and milk in mine, and when I thought she wasn't looking, I would pop another sugar cube in my mouth. She would laugh and say, "You are already sweet enough."

I loved her.

Now that she is gone, I remember these things. I close my eyes and it's like we are doing the things we used to do. Sometimes the memories make me cry, and I wish she were really here with me. I miss her a lot.

But mostly when I think about her I remember our time together and smile. I get a warm fuzzy feeling in my stomach. When I get that warm feeling deep within me, it makes me know for sure, I loved her.